14 Days

W9-BAJ-222

THE EMPTY LOT

BY

DALE H. FIFE

WITH PICTURES BY

JIM ARNOSKY

Harry Hale owns a vacant lot that he hasn't visited for years. "What good is an empty lot?" he thinks, and he makes up his mind to sell it. But when Harry visits his lot to decide on a price, he's surprised to find that it's far from empty. In fact, his little patch of land is bursting with life.

Dale Fife's engaging story and Jim Arnosky's lighthearted illustrations work in perfect harmony to show how, little by little, the gentle charms of nature overcome Harry's citified notions. Children of all ages will delight in Harry's unexpected discoveries and share his newfound respect for the many living creatures to whom an "empty" lot is home.

THE
EMPTY LOT

THE EMPTY LOT
BY
DALE H. FIFE

WITH PICTURES BY

JIM ARNOSKY

Sierra Club Books | Little, Brown and Company

San Francisco | Boston • Toronto • London

The Sierra Club, founded in 1892 by John Muir, has devoted itself to the study and protection of the earth's scenic and ecological resources — mountains, wetlands, woodlands, wild shores and rivers, deserts and plains. The publishing program of the Sierra Club offers books to the public as a nonprofit educational service in the hope that they may enlarge the public's understanding of the Club's basic concerns. The Sierra Club has some sixty chapters in the United States and in Canada. For information about how you may participate in its programs to preserve wilderness and the quality of life, please address inquiries to Sierra Club, 730 Polk Street, San Francisco, CA 94109.

First Edition

Library of Congress Cataloging-in-Publication Data

Fife, Dale.
    The empty lot / by Dale H. Fife ; illustrated by Jim Arnosky —1st ed.
    p. cm.
    Summary: Inspecting an empty, partially wooded lot before selling it,
Harry finds it occupied by birds, insects, and other small animals.
    ISBN 0-316-28167-0
    [1. Nature — Fiction.] I. Arnosky, Jim, ill. II. Title.
PZ7.F4793Em   1991
[E] — dc20   90-8590

Sierra Club Books/Little, Brown children's books are published
by Little, Brown and Company (Inc.) in association
with Sierra Club Books.

10 9 8 7 6 5 4 3 2 1

LB

Published simultaneously in Canada by
Little, Brown & Company (Canada) Limited

Printed in the United States of America

Remembering the Ohio countryside and the Stieber woods — DHF

Harry Hale owned an empty lot. For years he had been too busy to visit the two acres of woods and meadow that had once been part of his grandfather's farm.

One day Harry sat in his office on the fortieth floor of a building in the big city, and he thought, "What good is an empty lot?"

So he ordered a sign to be put up:

FOR SALE

EMPTY LOT

Right away, three people wanted to buy it.

So Harry got in his car, and he drove a long, long way to see the empty lot before deciding how much to sell it for.

He was surprised to see that the little town he remembered had grown up all around his empty lot. Where once there were wheat fields, now there were factories and filling stations, houses and shops, schools and churches.

Harry started to unlock the gate in the fence that surrounded the empty lot when he heard:

"*Tap . . . tap . . . tap.*"

"Who's there?" Harry asked.

No one answered.

Harry closed the gate behind him and made his way through wild grass and underbrush.

The day was warm and Harry was puffing a little, so he sat in the shade of a buckeye tree. He took from his coat pocket the list of people who wanted to buy the lot.

"*Tap . . . tap . . . tap . . .*," he heard again.

It was coming from an old pine tree just a few feet away from where Harry was sitting. He got to his feet and peered up into it. He saw a woodpecker perched on the trunk.

"*Wick-up . . . Wick-up . . . Wick-up,*" the woodpecker said.

"Wick-up yourself," Harry answered.

The woodpecker flew to the topmost branch. He drummed on the tree with his bill, making a loud staccato noise.

Harry noticed that the woodpecker had made so many holes in the tree trunk that it looked like a high-rise apartment building.

A squirrel stuck its head out of one of the holes.

A chickadee complained from another: "*Dee-dee-dee.*"

"Ah, I see — tenants," Harry said.

The squirrel flipped its bushy red tail at Harry and ran up the tree.

The chickadee flexed its wings and flew away.

"*Wick-up . . . Wickupwickupwickupwickup,*" the woodpecker scolded.

"Okay," Harry said. "I can take a hint." He walked away from the pine tree and sat on an ivy-covered boulder and began looking at the list of names again.

Plunk!

An acorn just missed Harry's head. He jumped to his feet and the piece of paper fell from his hands. Overhead, a bluejay spiraled. "*Check-check-check,*" it cried.

"So it's yours," Harry said, backing away as the jay swooped down for the nut. It flew so close to Harry that he backed right into an elderberry bush.

At that, a sparrow flew out of the bush and into a nearby tree. "*Tchunk, tchunk, tchunk,*" it scolded.

Harry heard a faint chirping coming from the bush, so he stuck his head into it. There he saw three baby sparrows, mouths open, in a downy nest of grass. He backed out of the bush, brushing leaves from his hat.

"I see," he said to the mother sparrow. "It's your family."

The mother sparrow kept on scolding: "*Tchunk, tchunk, tchunk.*"

"Okay, I'm leaving," said Harry.

He stood at a distance, watching, waiting for the mother sparrow to return to the nest. She didn't. Harry wondered if she would. He had heard that sometimes birds abandoned a nest that had been visited by humans.

Then Harry heard a sound that made him smile:

"*Croak. Croak. Croak.*"

He followed it through ferns and wild grapevines to a stream at the edge of the lot. A frog jumped into the shallow water at his approach.

Purple-black dragonflies with iridescent wings hovered over the stream where water striders and beetles skittered.

Harry teetered on a loose rock. A salamander slid out from under it, and three bugs scurried for cover.

A fat toad blinked beady eyes at Harry. A mosquito bit him on the neck.

Harry unbuttoned his collar, rolled up his sleeves, and sat down under an oak tree. He thought about the offers he had to buy the lot. One person wanted to use it for a gasoline storage tank, another to enlarge his factory. The third wanted it for parking.

It would not take long to clear the lot. In a few hours' time, bulldozers would push over and uproot the trees. The big blade would scoop up underbrush, rocks, and roots. The lot would be bare as a billiard ball.

Harry felt in his jacket pocket for the names of the would-be buyers. The paper wasn't there.

Harry felt tired. He closed his eyes. He listened. He heard the twittering of birds, the droning of honeybees, the buzz of insects. Thousands? Millions? He heard the scurrying of small bodies in the brush. When he opened his eyes, a family of quail was parading, single file, right by his shoes.

A cricket was chirping somewhere nearby, and a spider was doing acrobatics as it climbed down from the oak on its thread.

The earth beneath Harry's feet was alive. Pulsing. Harry watched a line of ants crawl in and out of their ant-mountain home. He thought about beetles and fungi and molds, earthworms, and minute bacteria deep in the soil. He wondered how many wild things were watching him, mice and owls and hawks, from the jungle of a nearby blackberry thicket.

And then Harry heard the voices of children.

He got to his feet and climbed into a fork in the oak. From there he could see planks overhead. He puffed and puffed, but he made it to the makeshift treehouse.

Below, a group of boys and girls leaped over the fence. Laughing and shouting, they ran under the trees and swung from low branches. They picked daisies and Johnny-jump-ups.

A boy scattered crumbs from his lunch box, then moved away to watch the birds swoop down to eat them.

One of the girls plucked a blade of grass, put it to her lips, and made a whistling sound.

Before long, they all ran, whooping, out of sight.

Harry climbed down from the tree and walked back through the woodlot, the way he had come. He passed the elderberry bush where he had seen the sparrow's nest. He stood at a distance. The mother was flying in and out of the bush, bringing bugs and worms. She had come back. Harry smiled.

When Harry reached the big boulder, he saw that the list of buyers had fallen onto a patch of ivy. He picked it up. A snail was clinging to it.

"You're an educated snail, I see," Harry said. "A snail who reads my mail."

He brushed the snail into the ivy and looked at the paper. The snail had eaten the names off the list. Fine thing!

"*Tap . . . tap . . . tap . . .*" came again from the old pine.

Harry walked over and stood looking up at the woodpecker.

"*Wick-up . . . Wick-up . . . ,*" the woodpecker called.

"I hear you," Harry said. "I'm leaving."

Harry walked to the gate at the entrance of the lot and stood
for a moment looking at the sign.

He took a marker from his pocket and crossed out the
word "EMPTY."

Now the sign read:

Harry grinned and wrote in the word "OCCUPIED."

Harry thought for a moment about all the things he could buy with the money from selling the lot.

Then he took a firm grip on his pen and crossed out "FOR SALE."

Now the sign read just "OCCUPIED LOT."

Harry smiled and added: "P.S. EVERY SQUARE INCH IN USE."

The End